For Benedicte Barford and Stephanie Amster,
with love and thanks, Emma

First U.S. Edition: August 2010
First published in February 2009 by Orchard Books, a division of Hachette Children's Books, London

Little, Brown and Company

Hachette Book Group
237 Park Avenue, New York, NY 10017
Visit our website at www.lb-kids.com

Little, Brown and Company is a division of Hachette Book Group, Inc.
The Little, Brown name and logo are trademarks of Hachette Book Group, Inc.

ISBN 978-0-316-03674-0

10 9 8 7 6 5 4 3 2 1

WKT

Printed in China

I don't want a cool cat!

Emma Dodd

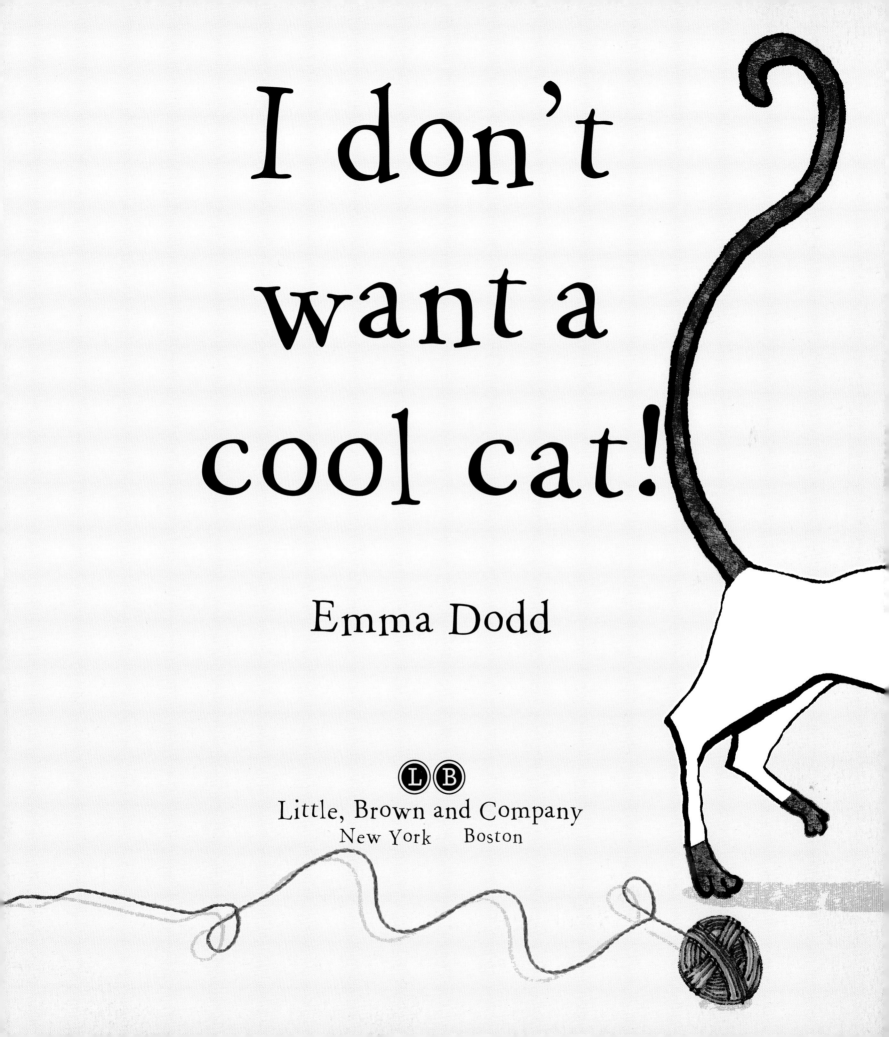

L B

Little, Brown and Company
New York   Boston

I don't want
a cool cat.

A treat-me-like-a-fool cat.

I don't want a stuffy cat.

A huffy, over-fluffy cat.

I don't want
a night cat.

A looking-for-a-fight cat.

I don't want a greedy cat.

A "Meow, meow,
        please feed me" cat.

I don't
want a
prize cat.

The best-that-money-buys cat.

I don't want a prowly cat.

A howly, yowly, scowly cat.

I don't want

a big cat.

Or a slinky,
dinky, twinky cat.

I just want

a purry cat.

A small,
soft,
furry cat.

Not a scratch or scrap cat.
A curl-up-in-my-lap cat.

A glad-

when-

I-come-

home cat.

A cat I call

My Own Cat.